Beast Quest

THE NEW AGE

SERPIO
THE SLITHERING
SHADOW

With special thanks to Allan Frewin

To James D. H. McLaughlin

www.beastquest.co.uk

ORCHARD BOOKS
338 Euston Road, London NW1 3BH
Orchard Books Australia
Level 17/207 Kent St, Sydney, NSW 2000

A Paperback Original
First published in Great Britain in 2012

Beast Quest is a registered trademark of Beast Quest Limited
Series created by Beast Quest Limited, London

Text © Beast Quest Limited 2012
Cover and inside illustrations by Steve Sims
© Beast Quest Limited 2012

A CIP catalogue record for this book is available from
the British Library.

ISBN 978 1 40831 845 4

3 5 7 9 10 8 6 4

Printed in Great Britain by CPI Group (UK) Ltd, Croydon, CR0 4YY

Orchard Books is a division of Hachette Children's Books,
an Hachette UK company

www.hachette.co.uk

SERPIO
THE SLITHERING
SHADOW

BY ADAM BLADE

ORCHARD

I heard of Avantia in my youth, when I flew with the other children over the plains of Henkrall. They said it was a land of beauty, bravery and honour. A place of noble Beasts, too.

Even then it made me sick.

I can't fly now. My cruel mistress, Kensa, was jealous of my wings, so she took them. Don't pity me, Avantians – it's you who should be afraid. Your time is coming. Kensa has plans for your green and pleasant land. Your Good Beasts will be no defence against her servants – they'll be powerless!

You'll need more than courage to protect you from the Beasts of Henkrall!

Your sworn enemy,

Igor

PROLOGUE

"I must be the unluckiest boy in
the whole of Northern Henkrall!"
groaned Idris as he stared through
the snow-laden fir trees that crowded
around him. "Why did I have to pick
the short feather?"

He and the other villagers had
drawn feathers to choose who would
climb into the sinkhole in the forest
to search for the Jewel of Journeys.
The legendary Jewel was said to give
its owner the ability to travel instantly

to anywhere they desired.

The others had not come with him to the mines.

He lowered himself over the edge of the hole. "I bet the Jewel doesn't even exist," he muttered as he began cautiously to descend. He had thrown a flaming torch down the hole to light his way. It flickered faintly, far below.

Idris folded his wings around himself as the mineshaft narrowed. He braced his palms and soles against the rough-hewn walls, creeping down step by step.

The torch was in danger of sputtering out. In this narrow space, he would be unable to spread his wings and fly if he lost his footing – he could fall to his death.

The chilly air in the shaft penetrated his folded wings as he descended. But at last, he landed on the floor.

He picked up the torch and stared into a narrow tunnel that jutted off at an angle.

Swallowing his fear, he made his way along the tunnel, his wings brushing the slimy walls on either side. The tunnel twisted and turned. He trembled, unable to shake the feeling that something – or someone – was down here with him.

Rounding a sharp corner, he was hit by a blast of freezing air that spun him around and around. His torch sputtered and went out, plunging him into darkness. He let out a yelp of alarm.

"I don't want the Jewel!" he shouted. He fumbled for the walls. If he followed them with his fingertips, maybe he could escape…

Another blast of icy air had twisted

him around and now he couldn't
tell which way he'd come.

He ran his hands over the walls
and made a choice.

"This way!" he muttered, moving
blindly forwards. "I'm sure this is the
way out. Ouch!" His hand touched a
wall of ice so cold that it burned his
skin. He sucked his fingers, turning
as another wave of freezing air struck
him. He stumbled and his wings hit
the wall of ice and stuck to the cold
surface.

Whimpering in fear, he ripped
his feathers free. A faint turquoise
light began to filter into the tunnel,
making the ice glow and sparkle.

Idris frowned, moving his face
closer to the wall. There was a dark
shape beneath the ice. Idris let out a
cry as a man's face came into focus,

the mouth open in a scream of terror, the half-spread wings frozen as though he had been trying to escape.

Escape from what? Idris wondered.

He turned, determined to escape that poor man's fate.

He gasped, as he stared into the source of the weird green-blue light.

It was an eye – a huge eye that stared at him from further down the tunnel. It belonged to something that was blocking his way out – a face that was moving slowly towards him.

Idris's wings unfurled as panic flooded over him. They struck against the walls of the tunnel. He heard the fine bones cracking, but he was too terrified to feel any pain.

The turquoise light blinded him, filling his mind with despair. He dropped to the ground, his broken wings folding protectively over his head.

He heard a soft, slithering, scraping sound. The thing was coming closer. He scrambled away from it, biting his lip to stop himself from screaming.

He got to his feet, but stumbled, hitting his head against the ice wall at his back. His vision blurred as he fell to the ground.

The eye came closer, and now Idris could see that it belonged to a gigantic serpent-like creature with a ridged skull and a slimy, segmented body so thick it almost filled the tunnel. The monstrous snake was coloured dirty grey and brown.

The Beast loomed over Idris, its vast mouth opening. It gaped wider and wider. He stared into the deep dark throat of the creature, too terrified to move.

A spurt of liquid ice sprayed out from the tips of the forked tongue, overwhelming Idris in a fierce rain of sharp droplets. He felt the ice flood his nose and fill his mouth, forcing its way down to his lungs.

As his body became encased in the hardening ice, Idris saw the turquoise eye staring at him in triumph. There was no escape.

CHAPTER ONE

THE GATHERING STORM

Tom stared into the sky. Dark clouds were moving northwards. A sudden wave of exhaustion swept over him. He hadn't rested since entering the land of Henkrall, and the effort of fighting the Beasts created by the evil sorceress Kensa had drained his strength.

He glanced at Elenna, hoping she

did not realize how tired he was. He shook his head, clearing the weariness from his mind. He would not falter, not on the first Quest since the death of his father, Taladon. He would battle in his father's memory. Failure was not an option.

"Igor said there was a storm coming," said Elenna, standing at his side. "If these clouds are anything to go by, it'll be terrible!"

Tom nodded. "The clouds are moving too quickly to be normal," he said. "I've got a bad feeling that Kensa has conjured this storm."

Kensa was as evil an enemy as Malvel the Wizard had ever been – if not worse. Tom had hoped that he had ended the threat to his homeland of Avantia when he'd defeated Malvel, but Kensa had arisen almost immediately. The Beast Quests had to continue!

Kensa had entered Avantia to steal blood from each of the six Good Beasts. She had escaped back to Henkrall and formed her own Beasts from her kingdom's earth, bringing new enemies to dreadful life with the stolen blood. But it wasn't only Henkrall that was threatened by Kensa's tyranny – she intended to take the Lightning Path back to the kingdom of Avantia and cause ruin and devastation there.

Tom had not hesitated for a single moment before agreeing to enter Henkrall to face Kensa. But the Lightning Path was a difficult road, and Tom and Elenna had been forced to leave their trusty animal friends, Storm and Silver, behind. The magic tokens that were attached to Tom's shield had been lost when he'd arrived in the new kingdom. But with each Beast that Tom defeated, a token had been returned to him: Nanook's bell, Ferno's scale, Epos's talon and Sepron's fang. Now, there were just two more to get – and two more Beasts to defeat.

Tom and Elenna were in the marketplace of Herrinfell, a village in southern Henkrall. They stood at the open doors of a warehouse belonging to Jaffrey, the village elder. Kensa had forced him to create a huge iron Lightning Staff. Her evil minion, the one-eyed hunchback Igor, had used magic to transport the staff to Kensa's castle. Tom feared that she meant to use its power to send her remaining two Beasts into Avantia.

"Remember what I told you," said Jaffrey, resting his hand on Tom's shoulder. "The Lightning Staff is harmless unless it has a jewel set into its head." He smiled. "There is no jewel large enough for such a huge staff – not even if Kensa delves in the deepest of our Northern mines."

Tom looked solemnly at the old man. "Kensa would not have made the staff if she didn't think she could find the right jewel," he said, turning to stare north. The Golden Armour he had left in King Hugo's Castle gave him the power of long sight. He could see dark clouds swirling and massing on the distant horizon. A storm was definitely brewing.

Tom turned his shield face-up. When he had arrived in Henkrall, a map had become etched on the shield, showing him the way forward in his Quest. He could make out a silvery path tracing its way across the wood.

"It can't be a coincidence that our path heads north too," said Elenna, leaning close. She followed the line with her finger. At its end, bright letters had appeared on the shield. The name of the next Beast. *Serpio*.

"We should go now," he said to Jaffrey, shaking the old man's hand. The other villagers had gathered around them. "I wish you well," he said. "And I vow to do all that I can to rid Henkrall of the evil that is rising."

"A party of brave people have already gone to Kensa's lair," added Elenna. "They might be able to overthrow her."

Tom nodded. He could only hope

his friend was right. A gap opened among the villagers and Tom and Elenna's new animal companions approached them.

"Are you ready for another journey, Tempest?" Tom asked, patting the purple horse's neck. Tempest lifted his head and whinnied, spreading his wings and striking the ground with his front hoof. Tempest may not have been a thoroughbred stallion like Storm, but he had proved himself brave and loyal.

So had Spark, the huge, shaggy wolf that now rubbed up against Elenna as she stroked his wings.

"Farewell!" called Tom as he climbed onto Tempest's back. Elenna mounted Spark, settling herself behind his wings and clinging to his thick fur as he leaped into the air and soared high above the village.

Tom grasped Tempest's mane
and the horse cantered across the
marketplace, his wings beating
powerfully. In a few moments, they
were in the air. The four of them
circled the village once, waving down
to the villagers, before turning to
the north.

As they flew towards the distant mountains, Tom gazed at the gathering storm clouds. Their next Quest would take them into the very heart of Kensa's storm.

CHAPTER TWO

SNARED!

They flew steadily northwards. Tom peered ahead, but the horizon was a grey blur under the seething clouds.

The moist air grew cold and Tom harnessed the power of Nanook's bell to form a shield against the chill. Elenna rode close, but Tom could see her lips turning blue.

"I don't think the bell has enough power to protect us all," Tom said.

"It'll be warmer on the ground."
He steered Tempest so that he glided
downwards. Spark flew down in their
wake, folding his wings as he came
along beside Tempest.

"It's not quite so cold down here,"
said Elenna, as some colour came
back to her cheeks. She pointed
ahead. "Where does that lead?"

A wide road stretched away
through the rocky landscape, twisting
and turning as it passed between high
shoulders of grey rock.

Tom took a quick look at the map
on his shield. "It follows our path,"
he said. "Maybe it will lead us to the
Beast?"

They followed the route, a cold
wind blowing in their faces as they
wound between the crags and
snow-capped peaks.

Tempest snorted and tossed his head, as though frustrated at being forced to walk, and at his side, Tom could see that Spark was also restless.

"There must be some villages in this area," said Elenna. "Perhaps we can stop and buy ourselves some warm cloaks?"

Rounding a bend by sheer cliffs, Tom was surprised to see the landscape falling away in wide icy plains. Beyond, a beautiful forest climbed the foothills of far mountains, the dense fir trees swathed in caps of pure white snow.

Tom checked his map. "Our path leads right through the forest," he said. Tom knew that the forest floor would be frosty and dark under those soaring, close-packed trees. He urged Tempest to a canter – the sooner they passed through the better.

They were at the edge of the forest when a voice boomed out.

"Halt, wingless strangers! None may pass."

A group of ragged people emerged from under the trees. They were winged Henkrall natives, but they had a wild and haggard look about them. Tom noticed that many of the men were wielding mining tools – picks and heavy hammers and iron spikes.

The women and children hung back, but the menfolk moved forwards, clutching their weapons, their wings spread. Tom watched the vicious-looking men.

"Perhaps we should try to find another way through the forest?" Elenna whispered.

Tom raised a hand in a gesture of
peace. "We're travellers," he called.
"We mean you no harm."

"You'll give us everything you own
before you pass through our forest,"
shouted the man who had spoken
first. He was large, with a heavy
beard. He pointed to Tom's jewelled
belt. "That should fetch enough

money to feed us for a few weeks!"

"There's plenty of meat on those animals," cried another with a spiteful grin, looking at Tempest and Spark.

"How did they get to be like this?" hissed Elenna.

"They're desperate," Tom replied. "We won't be able to reason with them. We need to get away. Follow me!" He tugged on Tempest's mane, turning the horse and urging him to gallop along the edge of the forest. Spark loped along at his side, Elenna clinging on grimly as the men chased after them.

"You won't escape!" one man howled.

There was more shouting. "Follow them! Bring them back!"

Tom glanced over his shoulder. The men were falling behind. The speed of the two animals would carry them to safety.

But then Tempest faltered, rearing up, neighing in panic, his wings scything the air. Tom was thrown to the ground. Before he could recover himself, Elenna came crashing down on top of him.

Both animals were writhing and straining against coils of ropes that had sprung out of the ground and wrapped around their legs.

"Our traps caught them!" shouted a voice. Tom looked back to see the men rising into the air on wide-spread wings.

Tom leaped up, pulling Elenna to her feet. "Into the forest!" he gasped. "They can't fly in the trees."

"But Spark!" cried Elenna, staring at the struggling wolf. "We can't leave him."

"We'll come back as soon as we can," said Tom, towing Elenna with him towards the trees. They had no choice – they had to leave Tempest and Spark behind for now. The winged men soared closer, their weapons raised.

As they ran through the forest, Tom heard the ominous snap and twang of a branch. A moment later, Elenna shrieked as her hand was torn out of his. He turned to see his friend snatched up by a trip-rope that had snagged around her ankle. It hoisted her up into the trees so she was hanging upside down.

"Elenna! No!" shouted Tom, darting towards her. But on his first step, he felt a rope tighten around his ankle. It jerked him off his feet, whipping him up into the trees. He writhed

as he hung upside down among the
branches. He saw the men coming
closer. He was at their mercy and
there was nothing he could do.

CHAPTER THREE

THE FOREST TRAP

Ice and snow rained down from the higher branches as Tom and Elenna hung helplessly, turning in slow circles. The rope was biting into Tom's ankle, numbing his foot, the knots drawn so tight that his skin burned with pain.

"Are you all right?" Tom gasped.

"Yes," groaned Elenna. "I think so."

Tom's head felt heavy as he hung,

gasping for breath. He stared down through the spreading needle-clad branches. The ground swayed dizzyingly below. *I have to get loose!* Tom thought desperately. *But how?*

Noise from below broke into his thoughts. More snow filtered down as the armed men pushed their way through the trees and gathered underneath them.

The men laughed harshly, brandishing their tools. But then pushing and shoving and quarreling broke out between them, some pointing up at Tom and Elenna.

"They're too high!" Tom heard one of the men yell. "Which fool set these traps?"

Some of them were trying to clamber up the smooth trunks of nearby trees.

"I think these snares were designed for heavy forest animals." Tom murmured to Elenna, seeing that her face had become red. "We're too light – we were pulled up too high. They can't reach us!"

"That's good," puffed Elenna, her face twisted with pain. "But how are we to get loose?"

"I don't know," Tom said between gritted teeth. He twisted this way and that, vainly trying to reach up to the knotted rope that dug agonizingly into his ankle. "I can't reach the knots!"

Elenna stared down at the wild men, bickering and quarreling below them.

"At least they can't fly up to get us in these thick trees," she said. "But that also means there's no chance of Tempest or Spark flying in to rescue us."

Tom writhed, kicking the air with his free leg, trying to swing himself over towards Elenna. He swung a little from side to side, but not enough to reach her.

He threw his arms backwards and forwards, swinging in a wider arc now. The blood pulsed in his aching head as he used every ounce of his remaining strength.

Elenna reached out and their hands touched and gripped. Now Tom could clamber hand over hand up Elenna's body until he got to the rope. Tom's muscles strained and burned with the effort.

"You can do it, Tom!" his friend cried as he hauled himself up the rope and into the branches.

Gasping for breath, his shoulders straining in agony, he hooked an

arm over a branch. Snow came down
all around him in thick clumps from
the higher branches. He could hear
the men yelling below. They could
see what he was doing and they were
angry that their prey might escape.

Straddling the branch, Tom began

41

to haul on Elenna's rope. He had to blink the sweat out of his eyes as he pulled her up. She reached above herself, her hands snatching for the branch, her face desperate.

With a final enormous effort, Tom managed to bring her onto the branch. While he recovered, she drew an arrow and sliced through their ropes with its head. But the branch dipped as it carried the weight of both of them.

"I'll move before the branch breaks," said Elenna, edging to the trunk and getting to her feet. She stepped to another creaking branch, but it cracked as she put her weight on it, and for a few moments she hung by her arms, her feet scrambling.

"Can you move to another tree?" asked Tom, watching her in alarm as she clung to the tree trunk, her face white.

"I'll try," Elenna gasped. She climbed to a thicker branch then got to her hands and knees and crawled along it to where it met the branch of another tree.

She reached out and transferred her weight. But just as she was about to pull herself towards the trunk of the tree, it swayed and shuddered.

"Be careful!" Tom yelled at her, but before he could do anything to help, he felt his own tree shaking so that he was almost thrown off the branch.

There was shouting and laughter from below. Peering down through the branches, he saw that the men had formed two groups and were heaving and pushing at the narrow trunks of the two trees. They were trying to shake Tom and Elenna loose.

"We need to get away from here if we can," Tom called to Elenna. He couldn't see her through the branches. "Elenna?"

He heard her give a stifled scream. A series of snapping and cracking noises followed, as though some heavy object was falling through the trees, breaking branches as it went.

"Elenna!" He got to his feet, clinging to upper branches as he swung himself towards the last perch he had seen her in. Freezing snow fell over him as he pushed his way through.

Elenna was nowhere to be seen. She must have fallen.

A gruff voice called from below. "We have your friend and we have your animals!"

Tom pulled branches aside to see

down. The bearded man was staring up at him. Close by, two men held Elenna by her arms, while others had tethered the struggling Spark and Tempest.

Tom let out a desperate groan. He was weary beyond words, and even if he survived this encounter, he still had a Beast to fight.

"Let them go and I'll come down," he called.

"I think not," roared the bearded man. "I am Niko, chief of the Forest Village. Nobody gives me an order! Come down now or I will kill the girl!" The man's eyes blazed with fury. "On that, you have my word."

CHAPTER FOUR

THE BARGAIN

"Step back, I'm coming down!" Tom
called. He leaped from the high branch,
dropping feet-first towards the men.
Startled, they scattered, dragging
Elenna and the two animals with them.

Tom landed easily. He drew his
sword, but held the blade low. "I will
fight you if I have to," he warned them.
"But I will not strike the first blow."

Niko spread his wings.

"No one attacks without my word!" he snarled. He pointed to Tom's belt. "We'll have that," he said. "See how the jewels glitter! It will buy us food."

Tom unclipped the belt and threw it at Niko's feet. "Take it," he said. "No jewel is worth shedding blood over."

One of the men scuttled forwards and snatched up the belt before running back to the others. A few gathered around him, examining the belt.

"The jewels are too small to be of any real value," said the first man. "A few days' food is all these will provide us with."

"If only Idris had managed to find the Jewel of Journeys," muttered another. "We would have fed our people for half a year on the proceeds!"

"The Jewel of Journeys never existed," said another. "Idris risked his life for a nursery tale."

Tom listened intently to their talk. Surely the Jewel of Journeys must be enormous to be so valuable. Perhaps it was huge enough to fit the great Lightning Staff in Kensa's castle?

"Where is this Jewel of Journeys?" he asked.

"What's that to you, boy?" asked one of the men.

"If I'm right, it's very dangerous,"

Tom said. "It should be destroyed before…" he hesitated. "Before it brings great evil."

"We'll destroy it all right," said Niko. "We'll break it into a score of pieces – each one of which will buy the things we need to save our village from starvation."

"Tell me where the Jewel is and I'll find it for you," Tom said. He was convinced the Jewel of Journeys was the one Kensa needed for the Lightning Staff. It was vital that he found it before she did. Tom pointed to Elenna and the two animals. "I'll trade the Jewel for my companions," he said. "All that I ask is that you break it into pieces immediately."

"We'll certainly do that!" said Niko. "And we'll be glad to tell you the way to the mine." He turned to the others.

"Come, let's give this brave lad
a warm cloak."

"My companions will have to
accompany me," Tom said, taking
his belt from the men.

Niko's face twisted in anger. "Do
you think me a fool?" he snarled.
"The girl and the animals will stay
here as a guarantee of your return.
Owain here will guide you to the
mines." A boy of about Tom's age
stepped forwards. He was dressed in
rags and streaks of grime ran down
from his fearful eyes.

"Very well," said Tom. "But my
friends had better be unharmed when
I come back."

He looked into Elenna's eyes. She was
angry to have been captured, but she
gave a brave smile. "You've never let me
down yet," she said. "Be careful!"

Tom nodded then turned as Owain
led him away through the trees.

They crunched in silence through
the snowy forest for some time, Owain
leading the way, his wings wrapped
around his scrawny body for warmth.

"How much further?" Tom asked.

"We're almost there," replied
Owain. "There's a mine shaft nearby
– the Jewel of Journeys is said to be
at the bottom."

Tom looked at him. "If your people know where the Jewel is, why haven't they found it?"

Owain gave him a shifty look. "The shaft is very steep," he mumbled. "It's dangerous."

"You people are miners," said Tom, now convinced that there was something he hadn't been told. He gave Owain a fierce look. "Is there something in the mine?"

"You know about the creature, don't you?" Owain breathed.

"What creature?" Tom demanded.

"I don't know anything about it," cried Owain. "But the legends must be true! Why else did my brother, Idris, never return?" He shuddered and tears ran down his face. "The creature killed him! The creature will kill anyone who tries to find the Jewel."

CHAPTER FIVE

THE BEAST IN THE MINESHAFT

Tom turned to Owain, his eyes
determined. "I've fought and defeated
more Beasts than you could even
imagine," he told the trembling boy.
"Whatever's down in the mine, we'll
deal with it."

Perhaps in the past the stories of
'the creature in the mine' had been
no more than scary legends – but

Tom felt certain that this creature was Kensa's next Beast, lurking down there, protecting the Jewel of Journeys.

"Take me to the mine!" Tom demanded. "There's no time to waste!" He had to find the Jewel before Kensa or her hunchbacked minion, Igor, arrived. At all costs, the evil sorceress must not be allowed to use it in her deadly Lightning Staff.

Owain ran on ahead, searching through the trees as Tom chased after him.

"Here!" the boy said after a short while. He stood on the brink of a round sinkhole in the snow. Tom stared into the small shaft. It was no wider than a wagon wheel, with rough-hewn sides that plunged straight down into darkness. Close by, an iron brazier glowed with burning coals. Owain stooped and unrolled a length of oilcloth. Inside were sticks bound at one end with strips of cloth covered in tar.

He pushed one of the sticks into the brazier and flames leaped up. Owain held the flickering torch out over the hole and let it go. Tom watched as it dropped, seeing it dwindle away

until it was just a bright dot in the darkness. It landed at the foot of the shaft in a tiny, faraway burst of sparks.

"We cannot climb down holding a torch," Owain explained. "This is how my people light the mine shafts." He straightened his shoulders, although his eyes betrayed the fear he was feeling. "I'll go down first," he said.

The boy's braver than he looks, thought Tom.

Folding his wings tightly around his body, Owain lowered himself over the lip of rock and clambered down into the hole. "There are hand and foot holds," he called up to Tom. "Just do as I do."

Tom hitched his shield onto his back and followed the boy into the mineshaft. He was glad to have the

shield to protect him from the sharp
edges of stone that jutted from the
walls of the shaft.

They soon came to the bottom. Tom
picked up the torch and peered down
a long narrow tunnel, drawing his
sword in readiness for whatever they
might find.

"I'll lead now," Tom told Owain.
"Keep close."

Waves of chilly air washed over Tom as he made his way along the tunnel with the torch held firmly in one hand and his sword gripped in the other.

He wondered what kind of Beast could lurk down here in this freezing cold mine. The way the tunnel kept turning at sharp angles, he guessed the Beast would need to be lithe and flexible. But how big could it be?

Another gust of icy air came slinking along the tunnel, chilling Tom to the bone. He swung his shield off his back, using it to fend off the worst of the cold. "It won't be easy to fight down here," he muttered under his breath, noticing how smaller tunnels branched off every now and then. "And the Beast will be familiar with the layout of the mines." He could be in for the fight of his life, deep beneath the surface of Henkrall. And he didn't have Elenna or the two brave animals to help him this time.

Tom turned a bend and saw that the walls of the tunnel up ahead were tinted with a pale turquoise light. As he approached the next twist in the tunnel, he saw that the light pulsed in a strange rhythm.

Could it be Kensa? Was she already here, lurking in wait for him?

He sprang around the curve. The strange light surged for a moment then faded away as a blast of icy air came rushing towards them.

The torch went out with a hiss. Tom felt Owain clutch at his arm.

"Be brave, Owain," Tom whispered. "Idris wouldn't want you to be scared."

"I know," the boy said, and Tom heard a new strength in his voice. "Carry on. I'm right behind you."

Tom discarded the useless torch, moving forward now into the faint turquoise light, sword ready, his jaw set and his eyes narrowed.

Owain let out a yelp of fright. A shed snakeskin lay coiled on the tunnel floor. It was ridged and dry, with curled up edges and a rough texture that rustled as Tom nudged it with his foot. Even withered up, the skin was more than twenty paces from end to end.

"A giant snake," Tom muttered to himself. Was that what Serpio was? At least now he could guess what he was up against. He rounded another bend and stopped dead in his tracks, his heart pushing up into his throat.

Ahead of him, half-filling the tunnel and bathed in the eerie glow, was a terrible sight! A winged young man was encased in a rugged block of solid ice, his face frozen in dread, his eyes staring.

Owain pushed forwards and beat his fists on the icy surface. "Idris!" he cried. "He's dead!"

"Stand back!" shouted Tom, raising his sword. He was about to aim a blow at the ice block when the blue-green light faded away. A blast of icy air hit him from behind. He turned as

the unnatural light blazed again.

A single huge eye glared at him, filled with the uncanny light.

Tom stepped back as the gigantic snake slithered closer, its jaws opening and a long forked tongue flicked out, tasting the air.

Tom had come face to face with Serpio!

CHAPTER SIX

EVIL UNDER THE GROUND

Owain let out a shriek as the huge Beast surged forwards. The single eye quivered and pulsed, throwing out beams of turquoise light as he stared at Tom.

A single eye! Kensa must have created this Beast from the blood she stole from Arcta the Mountain Giant, who also had only one eye.

Bitterly cold, stinking breath blasted into Tom's face as the Beast's mouth stretched wide and the long tongue flicked forwards.

Tom retched from the stench. Lifting his shield to block the worst of Serpio's freezing breath, he sprang forwards, his sword swinging.

The Beast jerked back as Tom thrust his sword towards the glistening eye. The long tongue wrapped itself around Tom's wrist, freezing him to the bone, numbing his fingers so much that his sword almost fell from his grip.

Digging his heels in and pulling back, he brought the rim of his shield down hard. The snake let out a fierce hiss of pain. The tongue loosened and drew back as Serpio shrank away along the tunnel.

"Owain – stay here!" Tom yelled as he ran. "I have to fight the Beast alone!" He chased the fleeing snake down the winding bends of the narrow tunnel. He could hear slithering sounds as it fled, as well as the hiss of its stinking breath. Moving fast, he rounded a bend, and was startled by a sudden darkness. The Beast was moving so quickly now that the light of its eye was no longer visible. Serpio had fled.

Slowing down, Tom felt his way along the tunnel in the deep darkness. Each of the Beasts created by Kendra had an evil heart – the source of its terrible power. But where was Serpio's? Tom wondered. He could not defeat the Beast until he found it.

He paused, listening intently, but he

could hear nothing. He was about to turn back when the turquoise light blazed out so brightly that it seared into Tom's brain, making him stagger back with a cry.

Serpio's great slimy body filled the tunnel. The Beast hadn't fled – it had been lying in wait for him, his eye closed.

How had he fallen for such a simple trap?

The jaws yawned and the long tongue slithered out again. But this time thick venom spurted from the tips of its forked tongue. Tom dived to the ground as the icy droplets splashed the walls of the tunnel, freezing and hardening in an instant.

I'm finished if that stuff hits me!

Now he understood what had happened to Owain's brother! He

had been caught in the venom spray
and been encased in ice. Tom rolled
forwards as the venom sprayed again.
The deadly gush of liquid struck the
roof of the tunnel, forming into a
gleaming sheet of ice.

Tom twisted onto his back, digging

his heels into the ground, pushing himself under the writhing tongue. He slashed with his sword, slicing through the flicking tips.

A high-pitched shriek came from the Beast as he jerked back, spraying a great fountain of venom and blood from his severed tongue. Tom drew his legs in under his shield as the spray came pelting down all around him like a deadly fall of hail.

Nanook's bell fended off the worst of the spray, and Tom leaped to his feet again as the Beast shrank rapidly away, letting out roars of pain and rage.

"Stay and fight!" Tom shouted, racing after the Beast. He could not let Serpio escape to do even more harm.

Something glistened on the floor

of the tunnel as Tom threw himself after the escaping Beast. It was the shed snakeskin.

Surely the Beast's own skin must be immune to the venom? Tom thought. He slashed at the skin, slicing off a quivering chunk that he threw over himself like a cloak. The skin felt rough and scaly to the touch, and it gave off a disgusting stench. But it would be worth it, if he could defeat the Beast and finish his Quest.

Serpio was slithering away from him faster than ever, the turquoise light dimming by the moment. Tom ran at top speed, but still he could not keep the Beast in sight.

A glint caught his eye along one of the side tunnels. He skidded to a halt, staring down a thin black shaft to where a small yellow light shone brightly.

Was this another Beast? If he passed it, would it come slithering out after him? Would he be caught between two deadly snakes?

But the light was different from Serpio's eye. Tom squeezed his way along the small, damp tunnel. A sudden hope ignited in his heart.

Brandishing his sword, he came into a wide chamber bathed in pure yellow light. The brightness was coming from the far wall. Tom walked forwards, narrowing his eyes against the glare. He stood in front of the wall, gazing at a huge shining jewel embedded deep in the rock.

"The Jewel of Journeys," Tom breathed, moving closer. It was beautiful, its many smooth facets throwing out beams of bright yellow light that shimmered over the walls

and roof of the cave.

Tom reached up and closed his
fingers around the jewel. It was just
big enough to fill his closed fist. The
light spilled out from between his
fingers as he took it down from the
wall and carefully pushed it into his
tunic. The yellow glow faded.

But a different light now poured

into the cave – evil, shuddering
and pulsing, spilling over him and
throwing his shadow across the
cave floor.

Steeling himself, Tom spun around.

Serpio's massive head filled the entrance to the cave.

He glanced around quickly, realizing there was no other way out.

Tom was trapped.

CHAPTER SEVEN

DUEL IN THE DEEP

Tom backed away as the gigantic snake slithered into the chamber, his eye glowing with eerie light. His mouth opened and the injured tongue flicked out, dribbling thick white venom that turned to ice as it hit the floor.

Keeping his face towards the advancing Beast, Tom edged around the cave, drawing the snakeskin closer around his shoulders, holding his shield up.

Serpio slithered further into the cave, his soft body oozing through the narrow entrance. His ridged head lifted, rearing above Tom, the eye filling with malice. A gush of venom poured from the tongue. Tom leaped aside as it splashed and hardened on the cave walls. Droplets of the venom rolled off the snakeskin, hard and smooth like frozen pebbles of ice.

Tom smiled grimly. He had been right! The skin was protecting him.

Hissing in rage, Serpio sprayed another gush of poison at Tom, this time throwing enough of the deadly liquid to drown him in ice.

He sprang upwards, the Golden Armour's boots giving him the power to leap over the gushing ice crystals. He gave one more great bound, this time jumping right over Serpio's head. The Beast slithered around, his entire body moving into the cave, his mouth gaping to swallow Tom in one gulp.

But the entrance was clear now. Tom made a run for the tunnel. Too late, the Beast realized his mistake. He lunged forwards, trying to prevent Tom from escaping. Tom spun in the mouth of the tunnel, lifting his shield and thrusting quickly with his sword.

Its point slashed across Serpio's eye, cutting through the glassy surface so that thick turquoise liquid seeped out of a long wound. The Beast roared in pain and Tom only just managed to avoid the gush of venom that burst from its tongue.

Writhing with pain, the Beast reared back and then lunged at Tom. But in his rage, he missed, striking the wall of the cave above the tunnel. The crash of the Beast's hard skull

smashing into solid rock echoed as
Tom took to his heels and raced away.
Shards and lumps of rock bounced
around him.

Everything was dark. Then the
rumble of falling rock died away and
Tom paused to catch his breath.

He drew the jewel from his tunic,
bathing the tunnel in warm yellow
light. Rocks piled to the ceiling behind
him. The tunnel was completely
blocked but he could hear thumping
sounds and angry roars, as the Beast
thrashed about in the cave, desperate
to escape. It would take Serpio some
time to burrow out of there. Tom
knew exactly what he was going to
do with that time!

He threw off the stinking snakeskin
cloak and made his way quickly back
to the main tunnel. He sprinted deeper

into the mine, searching for Owain.

He found him standing beside the block of ice in which his brother stood. Owain's shoulders were slumped and there was a hopeless look on his face. Tom could see a few scratches and scrapes on the ice, where Owain had tried to smash the frozen prison with pieces of rock.

Owain's eyes brightened as he saw Tom. "I thought you'd be dead by now!" he gasped.

"The Beast is trapped, but I don't think we have very long," Tom said, raising his sword. "Stand back!"

Owain moved aside as Tom aimed a blow at the ice block. Sharp splinters cut through the air as he hacked again and again. As his sword blade dug deeper, Tom became more cautious, picking and prizing the ice

away from around Idris's frozen body.

At last, a large chunk of ice came loose. Idris gasped and dropped to his knees, shivering and panting. Owain ran forwards, embracing his brother, his wings folding around Idris for warmth.

"Thank you," gasped Idris, his teeth chattering and his wings bedraggled with ice-water. "I thought I would be trapped for all time in that icy coffin."

"You're welcome," said Tom. "Follow me, quickly. We have to get out of these mines before the Beast escapes."

Idris stared at the jewel with wide eyes.

Tom nodded, knowing exactly what he was thinking. "Yes, this is the Jewel of Journeys," he told the brothers. "It really does exist!"

He led them back along the tunnel until they saw the distant daylight at the top of the shaft. Despite Idris's numbed fingers and toes, they quickly made their way to the surface.

"Go back to your people," Tom told the brothers. "Tell Niko to release Elenna. I'll need her help to defeat the Beast. Then

I'll come back to your village."

"Why would you want to fight the creature again?" Owain asked. "You have the Jewel of Journeys. Come with us."

Tom shook his head. "While there is blood in my veins, I cannot leave evil Beasts free to hurt people." He told them. "Now, go!"

Giving him a final puzzled look, the two brothers went racing away through the snow-covered trees.

"By the time Serpio gets free, Elenna will be here to help," Tom said to himself.

But a second later, he felt the ground vibrating beneath his feet. Twisting around, he saw Serpio burst out of the mineshaft in a shower of earth and stone, the enraged Beast roaring and spitting a fountain of venom.

CHAPTER EIGHT

TRAPPED IN THE TREES

Tom's sword rang as he drew it. He could see the thick slime congealed on the Beast's eye where he had pierced the glassy surface. But Serpio was staring straight at him – the injury hadn't harmed his vision.

The ridged head curved down on the sinuous body, the mouth wide to reveal long fangs. Tom took an involuntary step backwards, raising his shield to fend off the attack he knew was coming.

"Fool!" he muttered to himself. "You left the snakeskin in the mines!"

He glanced over his shoulder. The forest trees huddled closely together around the sinkhole. A huge Beast such as Serpio would not find it easy to fight among those interlacing branches.

Tom raced for the trees. He turned under the snow-laden branches and glanced over his shoulder. Serpio was slithering out of the hole, its body writhing from side to side as it came slinking across the snow towards him.

Tom's eyes widened – for the first time he could see the source of Serpio's power. There was a heart-shaped gemstone embedded in the

tip of the Beast's tail. Under the
stormy sky, it glowed with a fierce
golden light.

"It's exactly the same colour as
Arcta's feather!" Tom murmured
to himself. "If I can destroy that
gemstone, the Beast will be defeated!"

He brandished his sword at the
Beast then ran into the forest, hoping
Serpio would follow. His plan was to
run in a wide circle and then come up

on Serpio from behind, smashing the gemstone before the Beast even knew what was happening.

The Beast crashed through the trees, hissing and spitting, his deadly fangs ripping at the branches. Great flurries and clumps of snow cascaded down all around Tom as he ran. He glanced over his shoulder. Serpio was moving more quickly than he had expected, the long, lithe body slipping easily between the trunks, the blunt head breaking branches into splinters as it ploughed forwards.

In the gloomy twilight under the trees, Tom could see the turquoise light grow brighter as the Beast closed in on him. The tongue spat venom. Tom threw himself aside as the spray struck a tree trunk and encased it in a thick coat of ice.

Another gush of Beast-spit struck the ground ahead of him. He skidded on the sheet of ice, hardly able to keep his balance. His legs were aching with fatigue and he knew he was slowing down. Perhaps if he took to the higher branches, he would be safe from the Beast for a while.

He sprang high to catch a branch with his hands and swing himself up onto it as yet another spray of poison passed beneath him.Gathering himself, Tom began to climb up through the trees. He had never missed the encouragement and help of Elenna more than right now. Tom perched in the tree, peering down through the canopy of branches.

He could see the blue-green light moving around – Serpio was hunting for him. Then he felt the tree

shudder. A crunching, splintering
sound reached his ears. Serpio was
biting at the tree trunk, his sharp
fangs gouging out chunks of wood.

The tree swayed dangerously. Tom
clung on grimly as the tree began
to topple. He saw Serpio's mouth
gaping, the fangs ready to tear at
him as he fell. Tom leaped for his
life, managing to snatch hold of the

94

branch of another tree. But no sooner had he found himself a secure perch, than this next tree began to shudder and shake too.

"You won't win!" Tom called down. He swung himself from tree to tree, but always the Beast came slithering after him, cutting a swathe through the forest as his powerful jaws closed on the trunks and ripped the trees down.

Tom pushed a curtain of heavy branches aside and saw that he had come to the edge of a wide clearing. He turned, hoping to be able to clamber back to one of the trees that circled it.

But he was too slow.

He heard the sound of Serpio's fangs closing on the trunk of the tree he was in. The wood split and the tree toppled into the clearing.

Tom hurled himself forwards to try and avoid being crushed by the falling tree. He landed awkwardly, rolling over and over through the snow, dazed and in pain. His sword was thrown from his grip. A thick branch came crunching down on his legs, the crushing weight trapping him. Agony flared through his body as he was brought to a jarring halt. He struggled uselessly, anxiety searing in his mind. *I can't move!*

As he sprawled helplessly on the ground, he saw Serpio slithering out of the forest. The eye blazed with light and Tom had the feeling that the snake's lipless mouth was stretched in a triumphant smile.

Serpio glided forwards, his head rearing up. His jaws opened to reveal

the deadly flickering tongue dripping
with icy venom.

Tom fought wildly to get free. At
any moment he could be entombed
in ice. Perhaps Serpio had won,
after all.

CHAPTER NINE

THE SECOND EYE

An arrow came flying from the trees.
It stabbed into Serpio's gaping mouth,
making the Beast rear away, hissing
and screeching.

Elenna had arrived!

She came racing out of the trees,
kicking up snow as she sped towards
where Tom lay trapped. As she
ran, she shot arrow after arrow at
the Beast, driving him back as the

sharp arrowheads stabbed into his shuddering flesh.

"My sword!" Tom cried, pointing to where it lay in the snow. Elenna scooped it up and thrust it into Tom's hand. Calling on the extra strength that the Golden Armour's breastplate gave him, he hacked at the branch that was pinning him down. It snapped with a loud crack. Elenna dragged it aside and Tom leaped to his feet.

"Into the trees!" Tom yelled. "We're too vulnerable out here in the open." Serpio let out a high-pitched shriek of anger as they pounded across the clearing. He seemed to forget the pain of the arrows lodged in his skin as his prey escaped. Serpio sped after them, huge body scything through the snow, its jaws wide.

"Avoid the venom!" Tom called to Elenna as they ran. "It will freeze you solid."

Elenna nodded, glancing over her shoulder as they pelted through the trees. Tom heard the familiar sound as the furious Beast spat his deadly poison.

The white liquid froze against tree trunks, turning them into pillars of jagged ice. Serpio was spraying venom continuously, turning the forest to ice all around Tom and Elenna. Frozen branches came crashing down, spiked with knife-sharp icicles. They leaped over them, trying to keep their footing on the slippery ground.

But no matter how quickly they ran, Serpio was always hard on their heels. Tom knew that one pause or one fall, and the splashing venom would turn them to helpless blocks of ice.

"Do you trust me?" he gasped to Elenna as they dodged in and out between the tree trunks.

"You know I do," Elenna cried.

"I have a plan," Tom continued. "But we have to split up for it to work."

The noise of cracking and falling branches was coming closer and the forest was bathed in turquoise light. Serpio was horribly near.

"What do you want me to do?" Elenna panted, jumping high as a gush of ice congealed under her feet.

"Make the Beast follow you," said Tom. "I'll do the rest."

Elenna nodded and Tom sped off at an angle into the trees. He threw himself behind a thick trunk, clinging to it, listening to the rapidly fading patter of Elenna's feet as she sprinted away. Moments later, he heard the crashing sound of Serpio pursuing her. The ground trembled under his feet as great branches plummeted in the Beast's wake.

Tom risked a glance from cover. He could see Serpio's long body slinking rapidly through the forest, sending trees crashing down on either side.

Snow was raining down all around Tom, shaken loose from the higher branches by the tremors.

He chanced another look. Serpio's head was out of sight now and the slithering body was narrowing towards the tail. Tom hoped to follow the plan he had come up with earlier – to circle the Beast as he chased after Elenna, and attack him from the rear.

His fingers tightened on his sword hilt. A golden light lit up the snow – the gemstone in Serpio's tail was almost in sight now. He moved from hiding, darting from trunk to trunk as he closed in on the whipping tail. He could see the gemstone, gleaming brightly through the trees.

Now! Tom leaped forwards, lifting his sword high, ready to slice through the long writhing tail. But at the last

moment, the tail flicked aside
and Tom's sword crunched down
onto solid ice, jarring his arms
and shoulders and throwing him
off-balance.

The tip of the tail whisked around,
smacking hard against the side of his
head, sending him crashing to the
ground. Dizzy from the impact and with
his ears ringing, Tom rolled to avoid
another blow as the tail lashed down.

Serpio's head was far away among the trees – how did he know where Tom was? And then he saw the explanation – the golden gemstone had become a gleaming eye. It stared unblinkingly at him as he scrambled to get clear. The tail rose into the air, the eye watching as Tom tried to circle it for another attack.

"Tom! Help!" It was Elenna's voice. She was in trouble. He had to act quickly. *I have to make the Beast attack me instead of Elenna!* he thought.

Serpio had to think he was weakening. He dropped to one knee, faking a grimace and letting his sword hang loosely in his hand. He watched as the tail whipped forwards. The Beast's eye was ablaze with furious intent. The plan was working! As Tom knelt in the snow, the tail began

to coil around his body. He lowered
his head, his arms hanging limply as
the coils tightened around his chest.
It went against all his instincts not to
fight back – but he knew this was his
only hope.

He fought down the fear as red
sparks exploded behind his eyes.
He could hardly draw breath. It
was now or never.

The very tip of the tail loomed
up in his face, the eye gleaming
with wicked pleasure as the life was
squeezed from Tom's body.

At the last moment before his ribs
would have been crushed, Tom lifted
his sword and used all of his failing
strength to thrust the blade into
Serpio's tail just under the eye.

The glowing orb wheeled through
the air, its light fading and dying.

The Beast's tail jerked and twitched,
the coils loosening so that Tom was
able to leap free. He drew a deep
breath, relief flooding his body.

From among the trees, he heard a piercing howl of anguish as Serpio's whole body began to writhe and flail.

The golden gemstone fell into the snow – but it had already changed. It had turned back into Arcta's magical feather.

Even as Tom stooped to pick the feather up, he saw Serpio's body drop to the ground. For a few moments the Beast writhed and churned, the head and tail straining upwards. Then, with a final shudder, he became still and lifeless in the snow. A moment later, he vanished completely.

Kensa's Beast had been defeated!

CHAPTER TEN
BITTER VICTORY

Tom placed Arcta's feather back into place on the front of his shield. He had now recovered five of the six lost tokens.

Elenna leaped through the trees. There were ice crystals in her hair and her face was white with cold, but there was a triumphant smile on her face.

"You did it!" she cried to Tom.

"I was down to my last arrow!"

Tom nodded, exhausted from the battle. "Now we have to take the Jewel of Journeys back to Niko's people," he said, lifting his hand to his chest where he could feel the jewel nestling safely under his tunic. "They will have the right tools to break it into pieces."

They followed the trail of Serpio's destruction to the sinkhole, then headed back to where they had first encountered the mining people.

The ragged and starving forest folk were gathered around a fire in their encampment.

"Here they come!" called Owain as he caught sight of Tom and Elenna emerging from under the trees. "I told you they'd return!"

Tom was relieved to see Tempest

and Spark tethered nearby. They
neighed and barked happily, delighted
to see their human friends again.

Tom strode up to Niko.

"Well?" Niko asked, his eyes
gleaming. "Do you have the Jewel?"

"I do," said Tom, drawing it from

his tunic. There were gasps from the forest people as the Jewel of Journeys cast its clear yellow light across the snow.

"Give it to me!" Niko spat.

Tom placed it in his hand. Niko gave a crowing laugh as he stepped away from Tom, lifting the jewel high into the air. "We have it!" Niko shouted. "Finally, we have it!"

The people murmured. Although they seemed glad that the Jewel had been found, Tom had the feeling that they were also worried.

Something about it frightens them, he thought.

A deep shadow swooped over the encampment. People were looking into the sky, pointing and calling out in alarm. Tom stared up and groaned to see a familiar figure flying down towards them.

It was Kensa, riding a hideous
mechanical vulture, its metal wings
clanking noisily. The evil sorceress
was tall and thin with flying red
hair and eyes as green as poison.
Her clothes were held together with
buckles and straps and her wide
cloak snapped in the wind, its surface
covered in weird magical symbols.

As she descended upon them, her thin-lipped mouth stretched in a cruel smile. The stench of sulphur filled Tom's nostrils as the clanking vulture's wings cupped the air.

"Run!" Tom shouted at the people, leaping protectively in front of Owain. "She will kill you all!"

"Kensa the Great will not kill her obedient servants!" howled Niko, raising the jewel even higher on his outstretched palm. "She will reward us!"

"No!" shouted Tom, jerking backwards as the mechanical vulture's beak snapped at him. "You fool! Don't you know what you're doing? You'll doom the whole of Henkrall!"

Kensa swooped low, leaning from the back of the metal vulture to snatch the Jewel of Journeys from Niko's hand.

"Thank you, Tom!" Kensa cackled. "I knew I could trust you to bring this prize to me!"

"No!" howled Tom, jumping up and snatching at the vulture's leg as it rose higher into the air.

He clung on grimly as the clanking vulture soared above the heads of the forest people. Hand over hand, he dragged himself up and closed his fingers around Kensa's ankle.

She gave a scream of anger as she tried to rip her leg away from him. Down on the ground, he could hear Elenna shouting and the frantic neighing of Tempest and Spark's wild howls. They were all desperate to help him, but the two animals were tethered, and Niko had thrown his arms around Elenna, holding her tightly as she fought to get free.

Kensa leaned sideways in the saddle, the Jewel of Journeys in her fist. She struck at Tom, the jewel cracking against the side of his head with brutal force.

Fighting the pain as he hung on with one hand, Tom drew his sword. He tried to jab it into the iron flank of the vulture, hoping to smash its mechanism and send it tumbling from the sky.

But Kensa aimed a second, harder blow with the jewel at Tom's head. His whole skull exploded in pain. Red flashes filled his vision. His fingers loosened from around the sorceress's ankle and he fell.

He struck the ground feet first, a bone-shaking pain jarring through his legs. As the vulture lifted higher into the cloudy sky, he could hear Kensa shrieking with laughter.

A shadow came over Tom as he lay gasping on the ground, winded and wracked with pain. It was Igor, Kensa's hunchbacked minion, his

mouth spread in an evil smile. "My
Mistress has all that she needs now,"
he croaked. "The storm is almost
here – soon she will fit the Jewel of
Journey's into the Lightning Staff and
use it to travel to Avantia!"

Grimacing, Tom struggled to his
feet. But the hideous creature had
already vanished. He stared up into
the seething storm clouds. Kensa
had also disappeared.

Niko released Elenna and she
turned on him, her face twisted with
fury. "How could you betray us like
that?" she shouted. "We were trying
to help you."

"Foolish girl!" Nico scoffed. "Kensa
promised to protect our village if we
gave her the Jewel of Journeys." He
spread his arms. "The village is safe!
What's the harm?"

"You've given Kensa the power to destroy all of Henkrall!" Tom shouted. He stared up into the rolling clouds. He had defeated Serpio, but Kensa had taken the Jewel of Journeys. She was now terrifyingly close to achieving her evil purpose. The Beast Quest was entering its final hours, and it seemed that all hope of beating Kensa was gone.

Tom clenched his fists, anger and determination boiling up in him. While there was blood in his veins, he would not rest until he had thwarted Kensa's plans and freed the world of her evil. If hope was lost, then he would fight on without it!

Join Tom on the next stage
of the Beast Quest when he meets

TAURON
THE POUNDING
FURY

Win an exclusive
Beast Quest T-shirt and goody bag!

Tom has battled many fearsome Beasts and we want to know which one is your favourite! Send us a drawing or painting of your favourite Beast and tell us in 30 words why you think it's the best.

Each month we will select **three** winners to receive a Beast Quest T-shirt and goody bag!

Send your entry on a postcard to
BEAST QUEST COMPETITION
Orchard Books, 338 Euston Road, London NW1 3BH.

Australian readers should email:
childrens.books@hachette.com.au

New Zealand readers should write to:
Beast Quest Competition, PO Box 3255, Shortland St,
Auckland 1140, NZ or email: childrensbooks@hachette.co.nz

**Don't forget to include your name and address.
Only one entry per child.**

Good luck!

Fight the Beasts,
Fear the Magic

www.beastquest.co.uk

Have you checked out the Beast Quest website?
It's the place to go for games, downloads, activities,
sneak previews and lots of fun!

You can read all about your favourite beasts,
download free screensavers and desktop wallpapers
for your computer, and even challenge your friends
to a Beast Tournament.

Sign up to the newsletter at www.beastquest.co.uk
to receive exclusive extra content and the
opportunity to enter special members-only
competitions. We'll send you up-to-date info on all
the Beast Quest books, including the next exciting
series which features four brand-new Beasts!

All books priced at £4.99.
Special bumper editions priced at £5.99.

Orchard Books are available from all good bookshops, or can
be ordered from our website: www.orchardbooks.co.uk,
or telephone 01235 827702, or fax 01235 8227703.

Series 11: THE NEW AGE
COLLECT THEM ALL!

A new land, a deadly enemy and six new Beasts
await Tom on his next adventure!

ELKO
LORD OF THE SEA

978 1 40831 841 6

TARROK
THE BLOOD SPIKE

978 1 40831 842 3

BRUTUS
THE HOUND OF HORROR

978 1 40831 843 0

FLAYMAR
THE SCORCHED BLAZE

978 1 40831 844 7

SERPIO
THE SLITHERING SHADOW

978 1 40831 845 4

TAURON
THE POUNDING FURY

978 1 40831 846 1

Series 12: THE DARKEST HOUR
Out January 2013

Meet six terrifying new Beasts!

Solak Scourge of the Sea
Kajin the Beast Catcher
Issrilla the Creeping Menace
Vigrash the Clawed Eagle
Mirka the Ice Horse
Kama the Faceless Beast

**Watch out for the next
Special Bumper
Edition
OUT MARCH 2013!**

Join Tom on his Beast Quests
and take part in a terrifying adventure
where YOU call the shots!

FROM THE DARK, A HERO ARISES...

Dare to enter the kingdom of Avantia.

A new evil arises in Avantia. Lord Derthsin has ordered his armies into the four corners of Avantia. If the four Beasts of Avantia can find their Chosen Riders they might have the strength to challenge Derthsin. But if they fail, the land of Avantia will be lost forever…

FIRST HERO, CHASING EVIL
CALL TO WAR, FIRE AND FURY-
OUT NOW!

www.chroniclesofavantia.com

NEW ADAM BLADE SERIES

Coming soon 2013

Robobeasts battle in this deep sea cyber adventure.

Read on for an exclusive extract of
CEPHALOX THE CYBERSQUID!

The water was up to Max's knees and still rising. Soon it would reach his waist. Then his chest. Then his face.

I'm going to die down here, he thought.

He hammered on the dome with all his strength, but the plexiglass held firm.

Then he saw something pale looming through the dark water outside the submersible. A long, silvery spike. It must be the squid-creature, with one of its weird robotic attachments. Any second now it would smash the glass and finish him off...

———

There was a crash. The sub rocked. The silver spike thrust through the broken plexiglass. More water surged in. Then the spike withdrew and the water poured in faster. Max forced his way against the torrent to the opening. If he could just squeeze through the gap...

The pressure pushed him back. He took one last deep breath, and then the water was

over his head.

He clamped his mouth shut. He struggled forwards, feeling the pressure in his lungs build.

Something gripped his arms, but it wasn't the squid's tentacle – it was a pair of hands, pulling him through the hole. The broken plexiglass scraped his sides – and then he was through.

The monster was nowhere to be seen. In the dim underwater light, he made out the face of his rescuer. It was the Merryn girl, and next to her was a large silver swordfish.

She smiled at him.

Max couldn't smile back. He'd been saved from a metal coffin, only to swap it for a watery one. The pressure of the ocean squeezed him on every side. His lungs felt as though they were bursting.

He thrashed his limbs, rising upwards.

———

He looked to where he thought the surface was, but saw nothing, only endless water. His cheeks puffed with the effort to hold in air. He let some of it out slowly, but it only made him want to breathe in more.

He knew he had no chance. He was too deep, he'd never make it to the surface. Soon he'd no longer be able to hold his breath. The water would swirl into his lungs and he'd die here, at the bottom of the sea. *Just like my mother*, he thought.

The Merryn girl rose up beside him, reached out and put her hands on his neck. Warmth seemed to flow from her fingers. Then the warmth turned to pain. What was happening? It got worse and worse, until he felt as if his throat was being ripped open. Was she trying to kill him?

He struggled in panic, trying to push her off. His mouth opened and water rushed in.

That was it. He was going to die.

Then he realised something – the water was cool and sweet. He sucked it down into his lungs. Nothing had ever tasted so good.

He was breathing underwater!

He put his hands to his neck and found two soft, gill-like openings where the Merryn

girl had touched him. His eyes widened in astonishment.

The girl smiled.

There was something else strange. Max found he could see more clearly. The water seemed lighter and thinner. He made out the shapes of underwater plants, rock formations and shoals of fish in the distance, which had been invisible before. And he didn't feel as if the ocean was crushing him any more.

Is this what it's like to be a Merryn? he wondered.

"I'm Lia," said the girl. "And this is Spike." She patted the swordfish on the back and it nuzzled against her.

"Hi, I'm Max." He clapped his hand to his mouth in shock. He was speaking the same strange language of sighs and whistles he'd heard the girl use when he first met her –

but now it made sense, as if he was born to speak it.

"What have you done to me?"

"Saved your life," said Lia. "You're welcome, by the way."

"Oh – don't think I'm not grateful – I am. But – you've turned me into a Merryn?"

The girl laughed. "Not exactly – but I've given you some Merryn powers. You can breath underwater, speak our language, and your senses are much stronger. Come on – we need to get away from here. The Cybersquid may come back."

In one graceful movement she slipped onto Spike's back. Max clambered on behind her.

"Hold tight," Lia said. "Spike – let's go!"

Max put his arms around the Merryn's waist. He was jerked backwards as the swordfish shot off through the water, but he managed to hold on.

———

They raced above underwater forests of gently waving fronds, and hills and valleys of rock. Max saw giant crabs scuttling over the seabed. Undersea creatures loomed up – jellyfish, an octopus, a school of dolphins – but Spike nimbly swerved round them.

"Where are we going?" Max asked.

"You'll see," Lia said over her shoulder.

"I need to find my dad," Max said. The crazy things that had happened in the last few moments had driven his father from his mind. Now it all came flooding back. Was his dad gone for good? "We have to do something! That monster's got my dad – and my dogbot too!"

"It's not the squid who wants your father. It's the Professor who's *controlling* the squid. I tried to warn you back at the city – but you wouldn't listen."

"I didn't understand you then!"

———

"You Breathers don't try to understand – that's your whole problem!"

"I'm trying now. What is that monster? And who is the Professor?"

"I'll explain everything when we arrive."

"Arrive where?"

The seabed suddenly fell away. A steep valley sloped down, leading way, way deeper than the ocean ridge Aquora was built on. The swordfish dived. The water grew darker.

Far below, Max saw a faint yellow glimmer. As he watched it grew bigger and brighter, until it became a vast undersea city of golden-glinting rock rushing up towards them. There were towers, spires, domes, bridges, courtyards, squares, gardens. A city as big as Aquora, and far more beautiful, at the bottom of the sea.

Max gasped in amazement. The water was dark, but the city emitted a glow of its own

– a warm phosphorescent light that spilled
from the many windows. The rock sparkled.
Orange, pink and scarlet corals and seashells
decorated the walls in intricate patterns.

"This is – amazing!" he said.

Lia turned round and smiled at him. "It's our home,' she said. "Sumara!"

———

Calling all Adam Blade fans!
We need YOU!

Are you a huge fan of Beast Quest? Is Adam Blade your favourite author? Do you want to know more about his new series, Sea Quest, before anybody else IN THE WORLD?

We're looking for 100 of the most loyal Adam Blade fans to become Sea Quest Cadets.

So how do I become a Sea Quest Cadet?

Simply go to **www.seaquestbooks.co.uk** and fill in the form.

What do I get if I become a Sea Quest Cadet?

You will be one of a limited number of people to receive exclusive Sea Quest merchandise.

What do I have to do as a Sea Quest Cadet?
Take part in Sea Quest activities with your friends!

ENROL TODAY!
SEA QUEST NEEDS YOU!